Blue Bay Mystery

The Alden Family Mysteries
by Gertrude Chandler Warner

THE BOXCAR CHILDREN
SURPRISE ISLAND
THE YELLOW HOUSE MYSTERY
MYSTERY RANCH
MIKE'S MYSTERY
BLUE BAY MYSTERY
THE WOODSHED MYSTERY
THE LIGHTHOUSE MYSTERY
MOUNTAIN TOP MYSTERY
SCHOOLHOUSE MYSTERY
CABOOSE MYSTERY
HOUSEBOAT MYSTERY
SNOWBOUND MYSTERY
TREE HOUSE MYSTERY
BICYCLE MYSTERY
MYSTERY IN THE SAND
MYSTERY BEHIND THE WALL
BUS STATION MYSTERY
BENNY UNCOVERS A MYSTERY

BLUE BAY MYSTERY

by Gertrude Chandler Warner

Illustrated by

Dirk Gringhuis

ALBERT WHITMAN & Company, Niles, Illinois

ISBN 0-8075-0794-6

Published simultaneously in Canada by General Publishing, Limited, Toronto.

57 59 60 58 56

Printed in the U.S.A. 40

Table of Contents

CHAPTER 1

Plans

One winter day Jessie Alden met her brother Henry in the hall.

She said, "Henry, I think Grandfather is up to something. Violet thinks so, too."

"What do you mean, Jessie?" said Henry. "Do you mean business trouble?"

"Oh, no! Not at all!" said Jessie. "I think he is planning something. He jokes with Benny all the time. And he smiles to himself when he thinks no one is looking."

Henry said, "I hope he is happy. What else have you noticed?"

"Last night Grandfather was at the telephone in the hall. When I came down the stairs, he stopped talking suddenly.

"Then the other day a strange man came to see him. He was a very big, strong man. I could hear his deep voice. He laughed all the time. Jolly, you know. Grandfather laughed a lot, too," said Jessie.

"Maybe you are right," said Henry. "I'll keep my eyes open, too. He will tell us if there is anything he wants us to know."

Henry did watch his grandfather after that. It was true. Mr. Alden seemed very happy. Once he started to say something. Then he stopped.

Then at last, one day in January, the same man came to call. Mr. Alden took him into the front room and shut the door. He took the stranger's hat and coat and hung them up. He gave him an easy chair.

The four Aldens would have been surprised to

hear what their grandfather then had to say to the stranger.

He said, "My grandchildren love to see new places. They love adventure. They love boats. Henry is the oldest, and he and Jessie go to high school. Violet comes next and Benny is the youngest."

The man smiled. "So they all like adventure!" he said.

"Yes, but best of all, they like to make something of nothing. Do you understand what I mean?"

"Yes, sir! I understand very well, Mr. Alden. I understand because I am just like that, too! I like to make a fine fish pole out of a stick, a string, and a bent pin. I like to make a plate out of a flat stone."

"That's exactly right, Lars!" cried Mr. Alden. "You do understand."

Lars thought for a minute. Then he went on. "I think you want your grandchildren to have an exciting time, but you don't want them in any real danger."

"Right again!" said Mr. Alden. "Shake hands, Lars! And now I'll call them. You can watch them when I tell them!"

Mr. Alden opened the door and shouted, "Benny! Get Henry and Jessie and Violet. All of you come down. I want to tell you something."

The four Aldens were soon in the front room.

"Jessie, Violet, Henry, and Benny, this is Lars Larson," said Mr. Alden smiling. "He is your friend from now on."

Lars shook hands with them all. He said, patting

the dog, as everyone else sat down, "And this is Watch. I know him, too."

Grandfather said, "Now I am going to tell you about a plan."

"I told you Grandfather was up to something," said Jessie.

"Did you, my dear?" said Mr. Alden. "Well, we are all going on a trip. Lars is going with us. He has already been where we want to go so he can tell us all about it."

"How are we going on the trip?" asked Benny. "On a plane? On a ship?"

"Both," said Mr. Alden smiling.

"And where?" asked Benny.

"We are going to an island in the South Seas," said his grandfather.

"Oh, boy!" cried Benny.

"I'll tell you all about it," said Mr. Alden. "I have to go to San Francisco on business and I thought it would be fun for you to go with me. Then suddenly one of my business friends said his company's ship was going to Tahiti about that time, and did we want to go along? We would be the only passengers. So I said yes."

"So we are going to Tahiti!" said Henry.

"No," said Grandfather. "My friend told me about his first mate, Lars Larson.

"Three years ago, Lars was shipwrecked on a beautiful island in the South Seas. The ship hit a reef and two men were lost. One of them was Lars."

"He doesn't look lost," said Benny.

"No, the two men landed on this beautiful island in a lifeboat. The others were picked up by other ships. Lars and the other man lived on the island until a ship came and picked them up, too.

"Lars has told me all about the beautiful island. It is very safe, for nobody lives there. There are no dangerous animals. There is water, enough food to live on, and Lars would like to go there again for a vacation."

"And we're going to this island?" asked Violet softly.

"Right!" said Mr. Alden. "The Tahiti ship will take us there, and come and get us on the way back."

"Oh, what a wonderful idea!" cried Jessie. "We do love to see new places!"

"And we love ships!" said Henry. "You knew that, Grandfather."

"Yes, and who else do you think is going?" asked Mr. Alden with a laugh.

"I don't know," said Jessie, laughing too. "We never could guess."

"Mike!" said Grandfather.

"*Mike!*" yelled Benny. "Oh, boy! My old friend, Mike Wood. I would like that best of anything in the world. Mike and I could have a neat time. We're just the same age!"

Henry said, "This is such a grand surprise. You say we are going to fly?"

"Yes, we will fly from here in New England to Chicago. We will pick up Mike there, and go on to San Francisco. Then we will take the ship."

"But what about school?" asked Henry.

Benny shouted, "Oh, we stay out of school! That will be cool! You can tell our teachers that we are going to the South Seas, Grandfather."

Henry said, "Everyone in your school will know about the South Seas in just one day, Ben."

Mr. Alden laughed too. He said, "Let me tell you about school. I began this plan a long time ago. I talked with your teachers. They gave me all your lessons until you come back."

"Do we have new schoolbooks?" asked Jessie.

Mr. Alden smiled and said, "Yes, the books are right on the table."

He gave each one a paper book. Henry's was dark green, with HENRY on the cover in gold. There was a violet book with VIOLET on the cover, a blue one for Jessie, and a bright red one for Benny.

"Better not look at them now," said Mr. Alden. "They are very interesting. Every day on the boat you will study these books."

"A Boat School, Benny," said Jessie. She was afraid Benny would not like this.

"A Boat School!" cried Benny. "That will be fun, but we won't have school on the island, will we, Lars?"

"There will be no time, my lad," said Lars. "You'll be busy finding something to eat. That will be school enough. How about a lesson right now? A boat is *not* a ship. A boat can be carried on a ship. Our ship is too big to be carried by another."

"Oh, I get it," said Benny. "Then we'll call the school a Ship School."

"Almost, Benny," said Lars. "A sailor would say, Ship's School."

"That's neat," said Benny, "Ship's School!"

"Is the island beautiful, Lars?" asked Jessie. "Palm trees and everything?"

"Oh, yes," said Lars. "That's why I want to see it again. I'm glad to spend my vacation there with you. We can go fishing, too."

"Fishing!" said Henry. "Ben and I love to fish."

"And Mike. Mike loves to fish, too," said Benny. "Good old Mike! I can't wait to see him. Grandfather, you know it's awfully hard for me to wait for anything. When are we going?"

"Next week," said Mr. Alden laughing. "I know you can't ever wait. So that's why I didn't tell you before."

"We'll have to pack soon," said Jessie.

"No, that's another thing," said Mr. Alden. He looked at Jessie, the perfect housekeeper. "You see you will need other clothes for the ship, and still others for the island. It is very hot there. So your Cousin Alice packed your summer clothes and they have gone already. You will find them on the ship."

"What a grandfather!" said Henry.

"Can Watch go?" asked Benny.

"Sorry, my boy. Let me tell you about Watch," began Mr. Alden.

"And now I know he can't," said Benny.

"No, he can't," said Mr. Alden. "Watch wouldn't like the plane, or the boat, or the island, really. Mr. and Mrs. McGregor need a watchdog and we don't. Mike can't take Spot either."

"That's good," said Benny. "No dogs at all. You can't go, Watch."

"Watch has gone to sleep on my foot," said Lars.

"That means he likes you," said Jessie.

"I'm glad of that," said Lars. Watch lifted his head. Lars patted him and said, "Goodby. I have to go now, Watch."

"Yes, Lars has work to do," said Grandfather. "We will meet again in San Francisco."

They were all sorry to see Lars go. He was already a good friend.

When Lars had gone, Henry looked at Jessie and Violet and said, "Aren't we lucky to have a grandfather who takes us on a trip, and helps us go to school just the same?"

Jessie smiled at her brother. She said, "I was thinking the same thing. What a lot of surprises Grandfather thinks of!"

But nobody knew then what the biggest surprise was going to be.

Not even Grandfather. Not even Lars.

CHAPTER 2

Getting Ready

The next week soon came and the Alden family sat eating breakfast. Mr. Alden said, "You will not go to school today, for we leave tomorrow. You have many things to do."

"What?" asked Benny.

Grandfather laughed. He said, "For one thing, Benny, look under your chair."

Benny turned upside down and looked. "Oh, boy!" he cried. He pulled out a little bright red suitcase.

Henry looked under his chair. He pulled out a green suitcase just like Benny's.

Jessie laughed. She knew what she would find. She did find a pretty blue suitcase, and Violet found a violet one.

"From you, Grandfather?" asked Violet.

"No, they are not," said Mr. Alden. "Your cousins Alice and Joe sent them to you. You will each need a small bag for the trip."

"What about old Mike?" said Benny.

"Well, old Mike has one too," said Mr. Alden smiling. "His is dark red and yours is bright red. I hope you boys won't fight over them."

"Oh, no," said Benny. "We never really fight. We just have fun. I can always tell mine because I like bright red. It is like the fire house."

"You can tell yours because it says B. A. on it," said Henry. "Probably Mike's has M. W. on it."

"Yes, that is so," said Mr. Alden. "Today you can pack the bags. Put in only what you really need."

"Our books for one thing," said Jessie. "I can

hardly wait to see what is in that new schoolbook."

"Yes," said Mr. Alden. He looked at Jessie and Henry. "Those books are really wonderful. I think your first lesson should be a letter to your teachers. You can say thank-you for all their hard work. Then later you can thank them again, when you see the books."

"What about Mike's writing, too?" asked Benny.

"Look here, old fellow!" cried Henry. "You worry too much about Mike!"

"I think he ought to do what we do," said Benny.

Grandfather patted Benny's shoulder. "You may be sure he will, Benny," he said. "Mike and I have been writing letters to each other for a long time."

"I thought I saw Mike's writing!" said Benny. "I saw it just yesterday when I gave you the mail!"

"That's right," said Mr. Alden. "Mike is packing his red suitcase this very day. When we land at Chicago, Mike will be there waiting."

It was very exciting to take the plane. It was a jet. Stairs were put in place against the airplane door.

The Aldens went up the stairs with their bags.

"The first time we ever went on a plane!" cried Benny to the stewardess.

She laughed. "You'll like it," she said.

Mr. Alden had been on a plane many times. He could answer all Benny's questions. At last the plane rose in the air. They were off!

"I'll bet old Mike will be scared!" said Benny.

"We'll soon see," said Mr. Alden. "We will see Mike in just a short while."

When the plane started to go down, they all

looked out of the windows. Suddenly Violet said, "There's Mike with his dark red bag!"

"He doesn't look scared at all," said Jessie. "And do try to be nice to him, Benny."

"Oh, of course I will," said Benny. "He'll love this jet! I'll tell him it will say woosh! and we'll be there."

Mike was delighted to see Benny again. The two boys sat together and talked all the time. Mr. Alden had a seat to himself and slept.

"Did you get a schoolbook, Mike?" asked Benny.

"Yes, I have it right in my new bag. Your grandfather asked my teacher to write it for me. It has lots of pictures in it, too."

"There! You looked, Mike! Grandfather said not to look until we were on the boat!"

"Careful, Ben!" said Henry.

"I didn't look very much," said Mike. "I just saw one picture of a big fish."

"A fish!" said Benny. "What a schoolbook! I suppose mine is different."

Soon they had lunch. Then the plane began to go down again.

"So many exciting things," said Jessie. "We don't have time to think."

"You will have plenty of time when you get on the ship," said Mr. Alden.

Jessie was right and Mr. Alden was right. They landed. They said good-by to the stewardess. Mr. Alden got a car to take them to the ship. The ship's name was the *Sea Star*, and they were soon on it.

"Here we are!" said Mr. Alden. "And here is your friend, Lars!"

Lars was in uniform.

"You look different, Lars," said Benny.

"Yes, my lad. I'm a sailor now. I'm still First Mate on this ship until we get to the island. This is Captain Brown."

The Captain shook hands with them all. He seemed to know all their names.

"This ship is very big, isn't it, Grandfather?" said Benny.

SEA STAR

Grandfather laughed. "Yes," he said. "It is not a passenger ship. It is a big freighter, but it's very clean and very safe. And it will take us where we want to go. Not many ships can do that, for very few ships go to that island."

"We want to go to a beautiful desert island, Captain," said Mike.

"And that's where we will take you," said Captain Brown. "You are the only people on the ship, except the crew. Lars will show you where you eat and sleep."

The boat rocked gently at the dock. Jessie and Violet had one very small room. Benny and Mike had another very small one. Henry and Mr. Alden each had a room to himself.

"We can take only eight people," said Lars. "The cargo takes up a lot of room on the ship." There was still room on deck for seven long chairs.

Soon there were six people in the chairs. The men shouted and threw the ropes over on the deck. The freighter began to move.

"Here we go!" sang Benny and Mike together.

They were chugging under the beautiful Golden Gate bridge into the great Pacific Ocean!

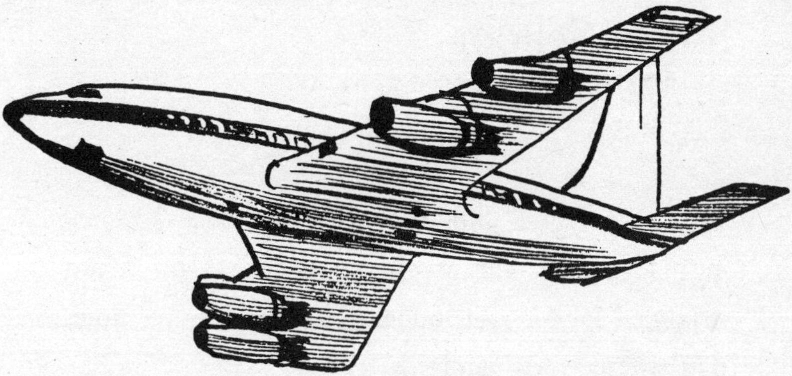

CHAPTER 3

Ship's School

Sea gulls flew after the boat, screaming. The cook threw out food for them. They screamed louder and louder. More and more came, until there were hundreds.

"Aren't they beautiful!" cried Jessie. She went over to look. A big gull landed on the rail near her. "They are such a lovely gray color."

"How long will this trip be, Captain?" asked Henry.

"About two weeks," said Captain Brown. "Then

we'll put the family off at the island, and the *Sea Star* will go on to Tahiti."

"Who is the family?" asked Mike. "Am I in the family?"

"Of course," said Benny. "I wouldn't go without you, would I?"

"Then the *Sea Star* will come back for us," Henry went on.

"Right. You will be alone on the island with Lars for two or three weeks. I understand that's what you want?"

"Yes," said Jessie. "We love to live like that. We like to find our own food and dishes, and we love to explore."

The sunset came then. It was beautiful. The whole sky was red and pink and violet. "We never saw anything like that at home," Violet said.

It was beautiful after the sun went down. The sky was black, but the stars were wonderful.

Benny said, "I never really saw the stars before. I didn't know they were so bright."

The Captain said, "You can see the same stars here that you see at home. Later you will see stars you never saw before. I will show you the Southern Cross."

Everyone was tired. They slept well all night. The next morning after breakfast a bell rang.

"What's that?" asked Mike. "It sounds like a school bell!"

"I think it is a school bell," said Henry laughing. "Look at Grandfather. He is ringing it."

Mr. Alden said, "School will begin at nine o'clock

every day. You can sit in your chairs and get your lessons. You will find things you need in this box."

In the box were pens, pencils, paints and all kinds of paper.

Jessie opened her blue book. "Well, well!" she said. "Here is Lesson One about gulls and stars and fish!"

"That's the picture I saw!" cried Mike. "It's a flying fish."

Soon everyone was busy reading. After a while Violet got up. She took a box of paints out of the box. She began painting a picture of a sea gull. Henry soon began making a picture of the Big Dipper in a black sky. The boys drew pictures of flying fish.

"A whale!" called Lars. Everyone rushed to the rail.

"It is very near!" shouted Mike. "Look at that tail!"

"There he goes, spouting water!" said Henry. A lot of water rose in the air. Then came the porpoises.

"There are about two hundred of them," said Lars. "They swim in a long line, like that, every day. They go over to one beach to eat fish and come back every night."

"Just see them roll around!" said Mike. "Are they round?"

"No. You'll find a picture of them in your book," said Mr. Alden. "I think that is in Lesson Two."

So it was every minute. The children saw something new and then they always found a picture of it in their books.

"I told you they were wonderful books," said Grandfather. "There is a lesson about the radio room. You will like that. Bill in the radio room will show you the radar tomorrow."

The next day the children saw every part of the ship. They knew every sailor on the *Sea Star*. They had school every day.

One morning the family could not see land any more. The bell rang for Ship's School and soon the five children were studying.

Henry went to the rail and looked down.

"Now this is interesting!" he cried. "Come and look!"

They all saw a long white bag. The ship was pulling it through the water.

"What is that thing?" asked Mike.

"It is a piece of cloth made into a net," said Henry. "It catches plankton."

"What is plankton?" asked Mike.

"It is made up of tiny, tiny animals and fish eggs and seaweed," said Henry. "Some of it is too small to see. But whales live on it."

Jessie said, "I've heard about it. I heard that we could feed the whole world on plankton if we wanted to."

"Why don't we?" asked Benny.

"People don't like it," said Jessie.

Mike said, "Maybe somebody will find how to make it taste good. Maybe I will when I grow up."

"Good old Mike!" said Benny. "Maybe you will. I'd like to see what is in that net."

The children looked up. Lars was coming. He said, "If you come below, we will pull in the net."

"Can we see the things inside?" asked Mike.

"Some of them," said Lars, "but some are too small to see. We have a microscope, which is fun to look into."

"Isn't this exciting!" cried Mike. He ran down the stairs.

A sailor had pulled in the net. He let the plankton run out into a big tub. The plankton was very bright colored. In the dark ship, it shone like red fire.

"Beautiful!" said Violet.

"How awful it smells!" said Mike.

"Just a good old fish smell," said Benny. "You'll have to learn to like fish, Mike."

"Oh, there's a tiny crab!" cried Mike. "I can see right through him!"

"And that's a tiny little fish!" cried Violet. "And pink seaweed. And green seaweed."

Mr. Alden had the microscope. He put it on the

table. Then he gave Henry a piece of glass. "Get some of the plankton on that glass," he said.

It was exciting when the glass went under the microscope. Henry had the first look. "After all, it's Henry's lesson," said Benny.

They took turns. There were many tiny eggs and weeds and fish that they could not see without the microscope.

Mike said, "So tiny! Tiny animals. Tiny everything. And to think this is what whales eat! They grow big enough!"

Benny said, "And now we all know Henry's lesson. That's Grandfather for you. He thought up this Ship's School."

The next day they all learned Violet's lesson. At first the school was very quiet. All were studying.

Violet surprised them. She was excited about something. She said, "Everyone listen to this! You've all heard of Captain Cook?"

"Oh, yes," said Mike. "He was the man who found hundreds of islands on his sea trips."

"Yes, Mike," said Violet. "That's what I thought. I mean I thought it was all he did. I can hardly tell you!"

"Take it easy, Violet!" called Henry. "You've got lots of time. What else did your Captain Cook do?"

"Thanks, Henry! It was really more important than finding islands. He found Vitamin C long before anyone knew what it was. Listen to this! 'On every long sea trip, more than half of every crew died of scurvy. Captain Cook thought they had scurvy because they had nothing to eat but salted meat and crackers. So he made every sailor eat sauerkraut and onions every day! They also had to eat a kind of syrup made of lemons and oranges.' "

"That wouldn't be too bad," said Benny.

"No, but some sailors didn't like sauerkraut or onions or lemons. And still they had to eat them. You see they got Vitamin C without knowing it. Even Captain Cook didn't know what Vitamin C was. He just knew people didn't have scurvy if they ate sauerkraut and oranges."

"I suppose that's why we drink orange juice every day," said Mike.

"Exactly right, Mike!" cried Violet. "Then when Captain Cook got home after three years at sea, he had lost only one man!"

"I bet that man wouldn't eat his sauerkraut!" said Benny.

"I bet so, too," said Mike.

Henry and Jessie looked at Violet. They both were thinking, "I never heard Violet talk so much."

But Violet went right on. "Then another thing!" she said. "Once he was sailing through cakes of ice, very far south. And he found that when he melted a cake of ice, it was fresh water!"

"That's funny!" said Henry. "I always thought salt water would freeze into salt ice. Then it would melt back into salt water!"

"It doesn't, though!" said Violet laughing. "Everyone else thought so, too. They didn't even try. Oh, Captain Cook was such a very smart man, and so brave! You all ought to read my book!"

"I think so too, my dear," said Mr. Alden. "I'd like to read it myself."

Day after day the *Sea Star* went along through the purple sea. It had been going for almost two weeks.

Mike said, "My, I'm hot, but I like it hot."

Lars said, "We are almost there, Mr. Mike. I think we had better get ready for our island."

CHAPTER 4

The Lifeboat

How do we get ready, Lars?" asked Benny, as they stood on the deck.

"First, we start to pack the biggest lifeboat," said Lars.

"We love to do things like that!" said Jessie. Her eyes were very bright. "What do we pack?"

"We must take a lot of food," said Lars. "Then we'll not have to live on bananas."

"Bananas!" cried Benny. "I'd like to live on bananas!"

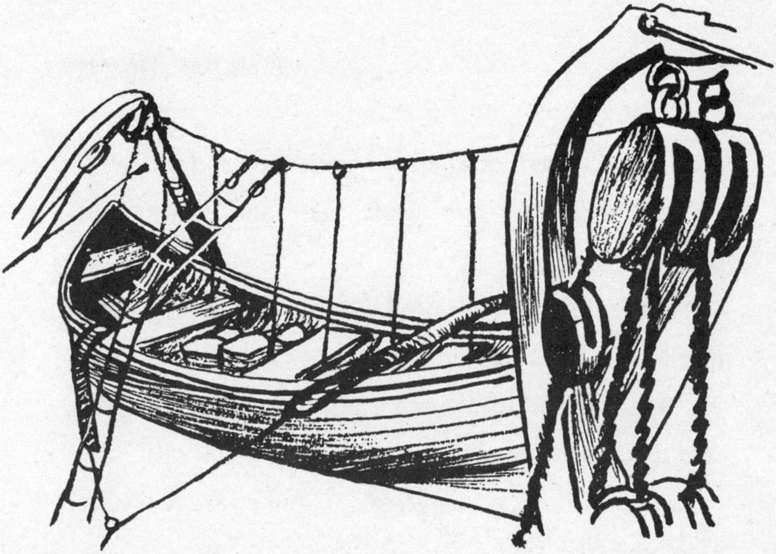

"Believe me, you could," said Lars smiling. "They grow wild. Just put up your hand and pick a banana whenever you want one."

"Oh, boy!" said Mike. "Come on, let's go!"

Mr. Alden looked at the children. Then he said, "Lars, you tell us all exactly what to do. You be the boss."

"Very good," said Lars. "I'll do that. Be sure to take shoes, and not little thin ones. You'll be walking over sharp stones and shells. Don't take any best clothes, but sport clothes. I'll pack the food we need."

"Oh, Lars, let me pack the food with you!" begged Mike.

"And me too," shouted Benny. "It won't take a minute to pack my clothes."

"All right, all of you can help. Come to the galley when you are ready."

Captain Brown laughed. "Don't forget seven blankets," he said.

"Is it very cold on the island?" asked Violet.

"No, it is very hot," said the Captain. "You sleep on top of the blankets."

Each one went to pack his small bag. Then they ran to the galley.

"Isn't it exciting?" said Mike. "I think this is nice!"

"I hope it will be," said Lars. "Now here is some dry milk."

He gave Mike a lot of little boxes to put in the big box.

"Let's have some beans, Lars," said Benny. "We all like beans."

"Just what I was going to say," said Lars. He was down on the floor beside the box. "Beans will do instead of bread. We can't take any bread."

"I don't like bread very well anyway," said Mike.

"Ho-ho!" said Benny. "I've seen you eat ten slices of bread at a time."

"And you, too!" cried Mike.

"Careful, boys!" said Henry. "Have a good time, but don't fight."

Jessie looked over the cans and boxes. "Let's take some cereal," she said. "That will last a few days."

"Here is some sea biscuit," said Lars. He gave Mike two tin boxes.

"Sea biscuit?" said Mike looking at the picture on the box. "I don't call those sea biscuit. I call them crackers."

"Even so, Mr. Mike, those are called sea biscuit," said Lars.

"O.K.," said Mike. "You call them sea biscuit, and

I'll call them crackers. Then I will know what I mean."

"Matches," said Henry quietly. He put some in the big box.

"Good!" said Lars. "We will need a fire, because we will catch fish and cook them."

"We will need dishes," said Jessie.

"Not too many," said Lars. "We can use leaves for plates. But take a big spoon and some knives. A hatchet, too, to cut trees."

At last the big box was ready. The children went back to their deck chairs.

"Watch, now," said Lars. We will soon see the island. Look out there, over the rail. It will look like nothing at first."

The children watched. For a long time they saw nothing but blue sea.

Lars saw the island first, but he said nothing. He looked at all the children to see who saw it first. Suddenly Henry went to the rail. "Is that land, Lars, or is it nothing?" he asked.

"It is land," said Lars smiling. "Soon we will see the green palm trees and the big round bay. I told you it looked like nothing at first."

Everyone went to the rail and watched the green spot. An hour or so later, they could see white sand around the edge. They could see the waves on the beach.

The *Sea Star* came nearer and nearer. They could see big palm trees bending over the water. The ship stopped. The crew began to let the lifeboat down into the water. They put in the seven blankets and the big box. The family and four sailors went down a ladder into the lifeboat. They all sat down.

Another lifeboat was fastened to their boat for the sailors' return to the ship.

Lars said to Henry, "You sit on this seat and watch how I use the rudder."

"All right, sir," said Henry.

Captain Brown called, "You can expect us in two or three weeks. But don't worry if we are late."

"I hope you *will* be late," said Mike. "It will be so

much fun on the island that we won't want to leave."

"I hope so," said the Captain, laughing. "And you all mind Lars. He knows best."

The men untied the rope, and the lifeboats started out on the big ocean. The boat tipped and rocked.

"Should we be afraid, Lars?" asked Violet.

"No, Miss Violet, not afraid, but we are all going to get very wet. Wet from head to foot."

"All right," said Benny. "But why will we get wet? Do you think we'll fall out of the boat?"

"No," said Lars. "You won't if you sit still. But when we land, you will all have to help. You will have to step out into the water."

Jessie said, "That will be all right, Lars. All our clothes will dry in a short time in this heat."

The family looked back at the *Sea Star*. It was getting farther and farther away. They all waved at Captain Brown. Then Henry saw that Violet had a large cloth bag in her hand.

"What's in that big bag, Violet?" he asked.

"A secret," said Violet.

"Oh, tell us!" said Benny.

"Oh, no, Benny," said Violet. "That is what a secret is. You don't tell anybody."

"Don't bother her, Ben," said Mike. "Violet can have a secret if she wants to. I don't even want to know, myself."

Then they all looked at the island. It came nearer and nearer. There were great rocks on one side. Palm trees were hanging over the edge. All around the water was blue, blue.

"I never saw such a lovely blue!" cried Jessie.

"You never will," said Lars. "They say this is the bluest bay in the world. We call it Blue Bay. Now take off your shoes and throw them in the middle of the boat. Be ready to jump out and pull the boat up on the sand!"

The waves were high now. Every wave took the boat nearer shore. Lars gave a last pull on the oars. "Now!" he shouted.

Everyone jumped over the side into the water. Mr. Alden surprised them all. He helped on the heavy end of the boat. Lars said, "Now!" The sailors gave a great pull as everyone helped. The boat slid up on the sand.

"Wonderful!" said Lars. "That was a fine landing!"

They were all soaking wet.

"Not for long," said Benny. "We'll be dry in no time. The sun is so hot."

"I don't want to get dry," said Mike. "I like to go in and out of the water."

The sailors climbed into the other boat and rowed back to the ship.

"Come here a minute," said Lars. "Benny, Mike and everyone come here!" He did not smile. When everyone was there, he said, "You must not go into this water any time you like."

"I know why," said Henry. "Sharks!"

"Right!" said Lars. "I suppose you have read about them." He was surprised. "I will show you a

fine place later, but we must get right to work. Now first thing! We must make a place to sleep tonight. We haven't much time."

The family stood on the beautiful white sand. They looked all around.

"What a beautiful place!" said Violet softly.

There were palm trees as far as they could see. Lovely flowers grew all over the trees. The flowers were bright red and yellow and white. The children saw trees and flowers and butterflies. But Lars and Mr. Alden saw banana trees, breadfruit trees and coconuts. As they looked, a great flock of blue birds rose in the air. Their big bills were bright orange. They did not make a sound.

"They can't sing," said Lars. "They are just pretty."

Then suddenly Mike shouted as loud as he could, "Two houses! Look! Two houses!"

CHAPTER 5

Food

At Mike's loud voice, everyone looked ahead. There were two old huts. The family started to walk toward them.

Mike got there first. "All broken down," he said. "No good after all."

Lars said, "Yes, they are broken down, Mike. But I wouldn't say they were no good."

"They are certainly better than nothing," said Mr. Alden. "Remember, we must have something to sleep in this very night. We have no time to rebuild the huts."

The old huts were side by side and made of bamboo and sugar cane. There were holes in the roof and sides. Lars went up to the first one and shook it. It did not fall down.

"I hoped these were still here," said Lars. "We can fix them before any rain comes, Mr. Alden. And we may not be here when it rains."

"How can you be sure about rain?" asked Henry. "It may rain any minute."

"Right. It may. I must work on the roofs tomorrow. We'll just fix the floors for tonight."

"How?" asked Mike.

"Do you see those tall ferns?" Lars pointed. "Get all you can, and bring them here."

The whole family began to pick the huge ferns.

Mike said, "They smell good, don't they, Ben?"

"Yes, delicious!" said Benny. "We can smell them all night."

Mike could hardly walk with his load. He threw them down in front of the first hut. "Now what?" he asked.

"Lay them all over the floor," said Lars. "They must be two deep. Then get some more."

They all worked very hard, but it was fun. They finished one hut and started the other. Soon that was done, too. Five blankets were put in the first hut. Two blankets were put in the other.

"That hut is for the girls," said Mr. Alden. "They have a whole hut all to themselves."

At last Mike stood still. He said, "Lars, I really thought the first thing would be finding something for us to eat, not picking so many ferns."

"Hungry, Mike?" asked Henry laughing. "Now you've got something there, brother! I am hungry as a bear. Where are those bananas, Lars?"

"Look over your head," said Lars.

"I see nothing but leaves," said Henry. "But what enormous leaves! They are as big as I am."

Lars smiled. "The bananas are behind those leaves," he said. "Just give me the hatchet." Lars was soon out of sight. When he came back he had a huge bunch of yellow bananas.

"Eat only one now," he said to the boys. "Then we'll start supper."

"Oh, what are we going to have?" asked Jessie. "I didn't know I was so hungry."

"Let's open the canned meat," said Mike.

"Oh, no," said Benny. "Let's save the meat."

"Why?" asked Mike. "Save it for what?"

"Oh, I don't know," said Benny. "Let's have beans." He looked at Lars.

"Yes, Mr. Mike," said Lars, "I think we had better have the beans." He winked and smiled at Benny.

"Why?" asked Mike.

"Because I like beans better," said Lars, smiling.

Benny and Lars were the only ones who saw the joke. They knew that there were three cans of meat and twenty cans of beans.

"All right, Lars," said Mike. "Certainly we will have beans if *you* like them better."

"Good," said Lars. "We must have a fire for beans." He looked at Benny and laughed.

"Do you want a lot of dry sticks, Lars?" asked Henry.

"Exactly right," said Lars, much pleased. "Bring them down to the beach."

Lars and Violet found some flat stones on the beach. First, Lars dug a hole in the sand. Then they built a little fireplace with the stones. Lars put on the dry sticks and lit a match. Soon the fire blazed high.

"Aren't you glad Henry remembered the matches?" asked Benny. He was kneeling on the sand, watching.

"Yes, we are very lucky," said Lars. "Now that's going to be a fine fire soon."

The fire burned well. Everyone put on sticks.

"Open the beans, Henry!" cried Lars. "Two big cans."

"Three cans!" shouted Mike. "I can eat one can all by myself."

"Think of tomorrow, Mike," said Jessie.

"No, Jessie! We can think of something else tomorrow," said Mike.

So Henry opened three cans of baked beans. Lars took the biggest pan with a handle. He put the beans in it and put it over the fire.

"Stir that," he said to Mike. "It will keep you busy. You sit and smell the beans." He gave Mike a long spoon.

"Now we need plates," said Jessie.

"Maybe you could find something," said Lars.

"I know," said Jessie suddenly. "Come on, Violet!" The two girls ran down the beach. Soon they came back with seven large shells.

"We washed them in salt water," said Violet. "And here are some spoons." She showed Lars seven long razor clam shells.

"Good," said Lars. "We can eat beans with them anyway."

"Not soup, though," said Mike.

"No, not soup," said Lars. "I'll tell you what would be fun. Everyone can make a spoon for himself. You can take my knife."

"I have a knife," said Henry.

"I have a knife!" said Benny.

"And me too!" shouted Mike.

"Now, don't forget me," said Mr. Alden. "So have I."

Violet laughed. She said, "Jessie and I will take your knife, Lars. But I am not a very good spoon maker."

"I'll make you one, Violet," said Benny kindly. "You might cut yourself."

"These beans are hot!" called Mike. "I'm going to take them off the fire."

Lars took the big spoon. He filled the seven shells. The family began to eat as if they were starved.

"Good," said Benny. "What else can we eat?"

"Milk and more bananas," said Lars. "Not a very good meal, but we can't have everything on a far-off island."

"I think it is a very good meal, Lars," said Benny.

Jessie said, "Violet and I found a fine dish-washing place." She ate the rest of her beans and began to eat a banana. "If you all wash your own shells, it won't be much work."

After supper the whole family went down the beach to the little sea pool.

Benny said, "No sharks can get in here, Lars. There are too many rocks. Right?"

"Right," said Lars.

Jessie said, "Now look down into the water. The water here is just like air. It's so clear, you can see the sand and all those funny things."

"Shells and crabs and colored fish," said Benny.

"That water is four feet deep in these pools," said Lars. "And see how clear it is. Jessie is right. It is just like air."

"Oh, look at that big fish swimming in!" cried Benny.

"That's a grouper," said Lars. "They get caught in these pools at low tide."

"Can't they ever get out?" asked Mike.

"Not till high tide," said Lars. "Low tide is the time to catch them."

"Here's where we go fishing then," said Henry.

"That's right," said Lars. "We can make a good fish stew with grouper and dry milk."

Jessie shook the water out of her shell. She looked at Mike. He was very quiet. "Time we went to bed," she said. "Mike can hardly keep his eyes open."

"Yes, I can, too, Jessie," said Mike in a loud voice, but he walked very slowly. When he reached the first house, he went in and curled up on his blanket like a little dog. Benny did the same.

Mr. Alden laughed and said, "Good night, girls!"

"Yell if you want anything," said Lars. "Remember now!"

Jessie and Violet curled up on their blankets in their own little house.

The whole family slept till morning.

CHAPTER 6

Surprises

Mr. Alden woke first. He lay very still. He thought to himself, "Breakfast will be strange for me. No coffee. I must learn to get along without my morning coffee." Then he went to sleep again.

Soon he was awake. He sat up and looked around. He was alone. Lars was gone, and the boys were gone. Then Mr. Alden smelled something. He got up at once and went to the door.

Down on the beach Lars had a fire. Henry and

Jessie and the two boys were kneeling down putting on sticks. Violet sat on a rock with a smile on her face. And what was on the fire? A coffeepot!

Mr. Alden walked down to the beach as fast as he could. Everyone began to laugh.

Benny shouted, "Surprise! Surprise! Aren't you surprised, Grandfather?"

"I never was so surprised in my whole life!" cried Mr. Alden. "And am I delighted to have my coffee!"

"So am I," said Lars. He winked at Mr. Alden. "I was going to give it up too."

Mr. Alden sat down on a rock. "Now which of you thought of my breakfast coffee? I'm going to guess."

Mike put his hand on Mr. Alden's knee. "You will guess right the first time," he said.

"Violet," guessed Mr. Alden. "That was her secret. The coffee and the coffeepot were in the big bag."

"Right!" said everyone except Violet, but she looked very happy.

Suddenly Benny said, "I see you opened the box of sea biscuit, Mike."

"I did not!" cried Mike. "I never touched the sea biscuit!"

"You didn't? Well, somebody did," said Benny.

"I noticed that, too," said Lars. He looked at all the children. "The box was open this morning."

They all said they had not opened it.

"Some of the crackers were gone," said Lars. He looked hard at Mike.

"I didn't touch the box, Lars," cried Mike. "Honest! *Really*. I don't like crackers too much. And I'd tell you if I wanted something to eat."

"Yes, you would, Mike," said Violet kindly.

But Lars still looked at Mike.

Henry looked at Benny. "Tell me, Benny, how did you know the box was open?"

"I couldn't have toast for breakfast," said Benny, "and I thought maybe crackers would be good. So then I saw the box was open."

"I never opened it!" shouted Mike.

"I know you didn't, Mike," Benny went on. "But Lars, you don't know Mike as well as I do. He would never take anything like that—never, never, never, never—"

"That's enough nevers, Ben," said Henry looking up. "We believe you."

"Lars doesn't," said Benny.

"No," said Henry. "But he will very soon. He doesn't know any of us too well, remember!"

Lars said to Mike, "I know you better now. They all stand up for you, so I know you didn't take the crackers."

"Good!" said Mike. "Thank you, Lars. I really, really didn't."

"Let's not talk about it any more," said Henry. "What are we going to do today, Lars?"

"We ought to explore the island," said Lars. "I want you to see the spring where the water comes from. Be careful of the coconuts. They may fall on your head. If you hear one coming from the trees, you must get out from under *fast.*"

Soon the shells and cups and coffeepot were washed in the ocean. There were no beds to make. So they all followed Lars into the dark, green woods where the ferns grew. It was a hard walk, and after a while Mr. Alden sat down on a rock to rest. He said, "You go along. I'll stay here till you come back."

"Won't you be lonesome, Grandfather?" asked Violet. "I'll stay with you."

"No, my dear," said Mr. Alden. He smiled at Violet. "You go along with the others. I'll be all right."

So they all climbed over the rocks and through the bushes until Henry said, "Listen! Water!"

Then they came to the spring. It was like a big round bowl in a rock. It was full of clear, cold water. The water came from a white waterfall which filled the bowl. Then it flowed over in another waterfall. Benny climbed above it to sit down. He found himself sitting on a beautiful curved rock covered with moss.

"Oh," said Violet, "what a beautiful big rock. Isn't

it funny? How could it come here all by itself? I don't see another rock anywhere around that's like it."

"Well," said Benny, "it looks like a great big enormous nose!"

Lars looked at it and said, "Benny, I think it *is* a nose. I never noticed it when I was here before. But I think it is part of an old statue. The people on Easter Island made hundreds of enormous statues. Nobody knows why they made so many. This looks like the noses on their statues."

"It fell down," said Benny. It must be very big.

This nose is twice as long as I am. Let's look for a mouth and some eyes."

Henry called, "I think the eyes are over here!"

"My, what a big statue!" said Mike. "Maybe a hundred feet long."

"Maybe," said Jessie. "I wonder who made it."

"I don't know," said Lars. "But this was a temple. You may be sure of that."

"Long, long ago," said Benny. "Let's have a drink out of the waterfall."

Benny drank first and then he climbed down from the big nose. As he did so, he saw a shell. He did not say a word. But he thought to himself, "What a funny place for a big shell. And it is clean, too. It looks like a water cup."

Benny left the shell right where it was. He said, "It's beside the white stone. I'll remember."

Just then he saw Jessie looking up into the tall trees. He looked up, too. The wind was not blowing at all, but one tree was moving. There was a crash, and down came a coconut.

"That's funny! Here's a coconut!" said Lars. "It isn't even ripe."

He looked up but he saw nothing.

He began, "Jessie, you know—" Then he stopped.

"What were you going to say, Lars?" asked Violet softly.

Lars looked at the gentle little girl. He did not want to frighten her. So he said, "Nothing, I guess. I was so surprised to see a coconut fall here. It is so dark in here that the coconuts are not ripe yet."

Mike looked at Benny. Benny looked at Mike. They both thought Lars was going to say something else. But they did not say a word. They did not want to frighten Violet, either.

"We'll go back," said Lars. "It is shorter walking on the sand than through the woods. Then we'll soon see your grandfather."

They did find it easier to walk on the hard sand. Sometimes there were piles of rocks, but it was fun to climb over them, too.

"There is another sea pool," said Henry. He bent over and looked in.

"Oh, *look!*" cried Benny. "Do look at this!" He was sitting on a rock looking down into the clear water.

Everyone jumped over the rocks and looked.

"What do you know!" said Henry.

The pool was filled with white sand under the clear water. But on the sand was a pattern of stones. In the middle was a beautiful white stone, perfectly round. There was a border of red stones around this. Four big pink stones were laid on the four sides. Between the pink stones were black ones. And around the edge was a beautiful border of three colors. These stones were red, white and blue, red, white and blue!

For a minute nobody spoke. And then it all came out. Benny said it. "There's a mystery here! That didn't just happen for nothing! Somebody made it!"

So at last everyone was thinking the same thing, "Somebody is on this island."

CHAPTER 7

Clues

The next day at breakfast Jessie said, "Lars, how about that fish stew today?"

"For Grandfather," said Henry. "He loves fish stew."

"So do I," said Mike. "All but the fish."

"You are funny, Mike!" said Benny. "What do you like, if you don't like the fish?"

"Well, I like the milk, and I like the crackers," said Mike.

Lars smiled at Mike. He said, "This will be the

day to eat the sea biscuit. Today we'll call them crackers."

Soon they all walked down the beach to wash their cups and shells. Benny and Mike ran around picking up colored stones and shells. Lars carried the tin box with the fish lines.

"Look at that great big shell sticking up," said Mike. "Come on, Ben, help me get it out." The boys dug the sand away with their hands.

"Oh, it's enormous, Henry!" cried Benny. "It's as big as a washtub."

Henry came back to look. "Lars!" he called. "It *is* as big as a washtub! What is it?"

But Mr. Alden was there first. "It's a turtle shell," he said.

"A turtle!" cried Mike. "I never saw a turtle as big as this."

"I have," said Lars. "That turtle must have weighed 300 pounds when it was alive. He was a big fellow. They grow big around here."

"Let's use it for a stew kettle!" said Mike.

"Isn't it wonderful?" said Violet. "We find a kettle the very day we make fish stew."

The boys went on digging. At last they took hold of the shell and pulled it out. It was full of wet sand.

"Let's wash my shell," said Mike.

"Oho! So it's *your* shell, Mike!" said Henry. "Well, I guess it is yours. You found it."

"We can all use it," said Mike. "I just mean I saw it first."

They all helped carry the shell down to the water. It was very heavy.

"Let's put it down here," said Jessie. "Let the waves wash over it."

They did so. And suddenly Benny shouted, "Look at it! Look at it!"

Violet called in excitement, "Come here, Grandfather! Look at Mike's shell!"

Lars said, "Look at that turtle's back, Mr. Alden, if you please!"

And there on the turtle's shell was a pattern. It was cut in the shell. It was exactly like the pattern of stones in the sea pool!

"Just exactly the same!" cried Benny, sitting down suddenly. "A big round circle in the middle and everything."

Jessie said slowly, "And now we *know* somebody lives here. This shell may be old, but the pattern in the sea pool is very new, because the tide would have washed it out to sea."

"Too bad we have to use this for a kettle," said Lars. "It is too pretty."

"Oh, no!" cried Mike. "I want my shell to be

a kettle. I'll always remember that I found our fish stew kettle."

"I think your turtle must have died, Mike," said Henry. "And then someone found the shell and made that pattern with a knife."

"Could be," said Lars.

"It could be the same one who made the pattern with the stones," said Jessie.

"You are right. Someone is here," said Mr. Alden. "But we must get on with our fishing, Lars. Let's pull this shell up on the beach. We can get it on our way back."

"Suppose we don't catch any fish," said Henry.

"Oh, we will! I know many places," said Lars. "Don't worry about that."

Soon they reached the pool. Lars said, "Take off your shoes and walk right in. Benny is right that no sharks can get in here. Sit on the big rocks. I'll give you each a fish line in a minute."

But it turned out that Lars had only four fish lines.

"It's just as well," said Mr. Alden. "You girls sit on the rocks and watch."

"Don't bother with these small fish," said Lars. "Wait for a grouper."

"There's a grouper in the pool now," said Violet. "He's a big one. He should be easy to catch."

Henry and Mike moved over near Violet. They let their lines down beside the fish. He lay still. Henry moved his line. Mike moved his, but the big fish did not bite.

"Well, let me try, too," said Lars. "Come on, Benny, we'll all try to catch him."

So there were four people trying to catch one fish. He began to swim slowly away, but he did not take the hook in his mouth.

"What do you know!" said Henry.

"Humph!" said Lars.

They waited ten minutes. They pulled the lines up and let them down again. Suddenly the fish turned and took hold of Henry's hook. Then he began to throw himself around. Henry pulled him in.

"Don't lose him now!" yelled Benny. "We waited long enough."

"He will do," said Lars. "He will make a big stew. We can catch more later."

They walked home. Henry carried the big fish on a stick. The children pulled the turtle shell as far as the fireplace and sat down. They waited to see what Lars would do next.

"First I'll clean the fish," said Lars. "He's dead now. I'll take off his head and his tail. And then I will cut him down the backbone."

"You take out his insides, don't you?" said Benny. "And throw them away."

"Right," said Lars. "There they go. Hello! Wait a minute! What's this?"

Lars took back the fish's stomach and pulled out a white button!

"Now will you tell me where that fish got a button!" he said.

"Somebody lost a button," said Jessie. "That's sure. Let me see it."

"It looks quite new," she said. "It's an American button, and it has four holes in it."

"It looks like a shirt button," said Mike. "Let's save it."

"Oh, yes, indeed," said Grandfather. "It's a clue."

Lars cut the fish into four pieces. He turned the turtle shell upside down. He put the fish into it.

"I like my kettle," said Mike happily.

"It's a good old kettle," said Benny. "Shall I put the water on the fish now, Lars?"

"Yes, it must cook for a while. Then the fish will be soft and we can cut it in smaller pieces, and take off the skin and take out the bones."

"I like onions in my fish stew, Lars," said Benny. "But of course we couldn't bring any onions."

"No?" said Lars laughing. He took some dried onions out of the box, and put them in the turtle shell. "I like onions, too," he said.

Suddenly a strange voice said, "Hello, Peter!"

"Who in the world is that?" whispered Benny.

Lars shouted, "Come out of the trees!"

The palm tree moved a little in the wind. They saw nobody. But all at once a little purple bird hopped out on a branch. It put its head on one side and said again, "Hello, Peter!"

"Well, well! A *bird!*" said Mike. "A talking bird!"

"What is it, Lars?" asked Jessie.

"I don't know," said Lars.

"I know," said Mr. Alden. "It's a myna bird."

"Oh, yes, it is, Grandfather!" said Henry. "Don't you remember, Jessie, we saw them on T.V.?"

"So we did," said Jessie. "There was a lady from a pet shop. She had two or three myna birds. She had taught them to say lots of things."

They all looked at each other. The bird said again, "Hello, Peter!"

Mike said, "Somebody had to teach this bird, Ben. Did you think of that?"

"Yes, I did," said Benny. "I think it must have been *Peter*."

"Yes," said Grandfather. "It must have been Peter, whoever he is."

CHAPTER 8

Cooking and Swimming

Lars was making the stew now. In the new kettle were the four pieces of fish, spring water, onions and salt. They all lifted the kettle over the fire. The children watched as it began to boil. Violet shook up some dry milk with spring water. After a while Jessie took out the skin and bones. She put in the milk.

"How are we going to eat this?" asked Mike. "It is boiling hot."

"I'll tell you," said Jessie. "We'll set our shells in

the sand. You fill them with stew, Lars. Then we won't have to hold them."

"Very good," said Lars. "I have made a fine ladle." The ladle was the tin cup tied on a long stick. Lars ladled out the stew.

"Don't give Mike any fish," said Benny. "He doesn't like fish."

"Well, I'll give him some just the same," said Lars. "He may get to like it."

"Now about Peter," said Benny. "Do you think Peter has been here, or is he here now?"

"Peter could be a name someone taught the bird to say," said Mr. Alden. "Then somehow the bird came to the island."

"It would be exciting if Peter were really here," said Henry. "And is he a boy or a man?"

"Oh, he couldn't be a boy," said Benny. "He couldn't live here all alone."

"Why not, Ben?" asked Mike.

"Well, he would be too lonesome. And how would a boy get here all alone?"

"Oh, I hope it isn't a cannibal, like those in *Robinson Crusoe*," said Violet. She looked up quickly.

"Oh, no, Miss Violet!" said Lars. "Don't you be afraid. It couldn't be a cannibal, because there aren't any cannibals on these islands."

Lars gave Mr. Alden a quick look. So Mr. Alden said quickly, "That's right, my dear. Lars knows. And just taste this stew!"

There were no spoons yet, but they used the razor clam shells.

Benny said, "My, you have to work hard to get this stew into your mouth."

"Makes it better," said Henry. "I am going to drink mine when it is cooler. And now what shall we do about this Peter?"

"Just keep your eyes open," said Lars.

"I kept mine open anyway," said Benny. "Let's catch the myna bird."

"We can't catch a bird," said Henry. "But maybe he can say other things." He whistled. The bird whistled.

"Now just hear that!" said Mike. He whistled. The bird whistled.

Mike got up and started for the tree. But the bird flew away at once. He was lost in the trees.

"Just one thing," said Jessie, looking at her gentle sister. "If Peter is here now, he must speak English."

"That's right, Jessie," said Mr. Alden. "A cannibal would not teach the myna bird to say things in English. And now let's think about something else."

"Well, I think I shall cook a breadfruit today," said Lars. "We will open some canned meat and have a real dinner."

"The stew is gone anyway," said Mr. Alden. "I had five shellfuls. Thank you very much, Lars. I enjoyed it."

Mike said, "I liked mine, too. The fish wasn't too bad. But the stew and crackers were the best. Lars, do you remember you said you'd show us a place to swim?"

"I remember it well, Mr. Mike," said Lars. "I will show you the place when we take a walk."

"Can you swim, Mike?" asked Benny in surprise.

"Well, I can swim a little," said Mike. He was laughing at something. "I like to swim, and it's so hot here."

"It is always hot in the middle of the day," said Lars. "We ought to rest, or else go into the woods. It is cool there."

"I don't want to rest," said Jessie. "Do you, Violet? Let's all go into the woods."

Nobody wanted to rest. They wanted to see the island.

"Just wait a minute," said Lars. "I will pick the breadfruit before we go."

"Where is the breadfruit?" asked Benny.

"Right over your head," said Lars. "I'll try to climb the tree."

Soon Lars came down with two large breadfruit. He climbed up again and came down with two more. He put the green fruit on the sand for them to look at.

"They look exactly like brains!" said Benny.

"Do they really, now?" said Lars laughing.

"How do you know what brains look like, Ben?" asked Mike.

"From pictures," said Benny. "Brains go in and out in a curly pattern, but brains are not green."

"I'll bake them," said Lars. "The fire is just right."

"I wondered why you didn't let the fire go out," said Jessie. "You kept making it bigger and bigger."

"Yes, we have to have a bed of hot coals for the breadfruit," said Lars. "Now I'll put banana leaves around them. Then we'll cover them up in the fire and leave them until we get back. Then I'll show you how to eat them."

"Will they taste like bread?" asked Benny.

"Some people think so," said Lars. "You have to get used to it."

"Let's go," said Henry. "We all want to swim."

"I want to see the place where there are no sharks," said Mike.

"So do I," said Mr. Alden. Everyone was surprised. Benny said, "Can *you* swim, Grandfather?"

"I think so," said Mr. Alden with a laugh. "I may have forgotten how, but I'd like to try."

"This is the way," said Lars. "It is quite a long walk, but it is very pretty."

They climbed over rocks this time. Once they came to a beautiful, white sandy beach. "Not here," said Lars. "There are sharks here."

"I haven't seen one shark yet," said Benny. "I've looked and looked for them in Blue Bay."

"Blue Bay is full of them, just the same," said Lars.

Violet said, "Isn't it lucky that Lars knows where they are!"

The family walked along the beach.

"More rocks," said Henry. "These are very big. Are you all right, Grandfather?"

"Yes, my boy," said Mr. Alden. "But I hope we will get there soon."

"We will," said Lars. "Take my arm."

Up they all went, jumping from one rock to another. Then Jessie said suddenly, "Oh, isn't this beautiful!"

Everyone stopped to look. Here was a green bay. It was smaller than Blue Bay, and perfectly round. All around the edge were palm trees.

"Trees growing right in the water out there!" cried Benny. "Just in a perfect ring. How can they, Grandfather? What makes them?"

"Those trees are not growing in the water, Benny," said Grandfather. "That is a reef. You will find a lot of land out there, but it is a beautiful sight."

Lars said, "This is the place to swim. The water is

not very deep here. See how green it is? Sharks cannot get in here. They can't get across the reef because there is no opening."

They all took off their shoes and walked into the clear water.

"Clothes and all!" shouted Mike. "Isn't this fun! I wish my mother could see me now."

"It's lovely," said Jessie. "It is cool, but not too cool." She looked up just in time to see Mike. He put his hands in front of him and swam off like a fish!

"Mike Wood!" shouted Benny. "I didn't know you could swim like that! I didn't know you could swim at all." Benny watched his friend. Sometimes Mike swam under water, and sometimes on top.

"Good work, Mike!" called Mr. Alden. And off he went, hand over hand, with his face in the water.

"Look at Grandfather!" cried Henry. "He and Mike are the best swimmers here."

But then Lars went after them, and there were three fine swimmers. Henry was just swimming on his back when he happened to look on the other side of the reef. He looked again. He stopped swimming and stood up. There was an old boat. It was pulled high up on the sand.

"Come back!" shouted Henry.

It was funny to see everyone coming back so fast Mike said, "Everybody minds everybody!"

"Look at that boat, Lars," said Henry pointing.

They all walked through the water to the reef. They looked across at the old boat.

"It is a lifeboat," said Lars. "But it was not there when I came here three years ago. I'm sure of that."

The boat was full of sand. One end was very deep in the sand, way out of sight. They all stood looking at the boat, when they heard a little noise in the tree above.

"It's a whine!" cried Benny, looking up. "Someone is in trouble."

The whine came again. But it was further away this time.

"It is just a little moan, now," said Violet. Then it stopped.

"Maybe someone doesn't want us to look at this old boat," said Mike.

Henry said, "Maybe someone thinks we are going to take it away. I wonder what it was or who it was?"

"That I cannot tell you," said Lars. "But this is a good boat. It must have a name. You all stay here, and I will walk across the reef and see." He looked at both sides of the boat, and there was its name, *Explorer II*.

"Oh, I know!" cried Lars. "This *is* a lifeboat. It came from the ship *Explorer II*. The ship hit a reef and went down."

"I remember that!" said Mr. Alden. "I read about it in the newspapers months ago. Some of the people were picked up by another ship and taken to San Francisco."

"I suppose some people got into this lifeboat just as we got in ours," said Benny.

After a while they all went back to the green bay. They swam around in the cool water. Then they came up on the beach and sat in the sun until they

were dry. The sun made them feel very sleepy.

"Dry in no time," said Mike. "That's this hot sun for you!"

"Now we'd better sit up here under the trees," said Lars. "The sun is too hot."

They sat down under the palm trees. Soon Mike lay down with his head on his arm. Benny did the same. The rest laughed a little, but soon they were all stretched out on the beach, too. Soon the whole family was asleep on the sand—all but one. Lars was lying down. But he watched the water and the trees and the beach. He saw nothing.

Even Lars did not know that anyone was looking at them from the tree right over their heads.

CHAPTER 9

Bread

One by one the family woke up. They laughed at one another for going to sleep on the sand.

"We needed a nap in the middle of the day," said Mr. Alden. "The sun is very hot."

"I'd like to see how that breadfruit is getting along," said Jessie.

"So would I," said Mike. "It doesn't look like bread at all."

"No, only like big green brains," said Benny.

Over the rocks they went. They walked along the

sandy beach. "We ought to call this Shark Bay," said Mike.

"Good," said Lars. "That is just what it is. It is very dangerous."

Everyone was looking at the water. All but Benny. He happened to look the other way. He looked at the woods. Something was moving in the woods. He looked again. A long vine was swinging. One end of the vine was up in a tall tree. The other end went up, too. It went out of sight in another tree.

"A swing!" shouted Benny. "Look at it."

"Now what do you know!" said Henry. "A real swing."

Lars walked through the bushes. He pulled on the swing. It did not come down.

"Here, let me sit in it," cried Mike. He sat down on the big vine and pushed. The swing seemed to be very strong.

"I can go way up high, Ben!" cried Mike excitedly.

"Be careful, Mike," said Grandfather. "Take it

easy. That swing might break suddenly. We don't want any broken legs here."

Henry said, "Grandfather, a vine wouldn't grow like that all by itself, would it?"

"It could grow like that," said Mr. Alden, "but I don't think it did. See, all the leaves are off. Someone took off all the leaves."

"Oh, dear," said Jessie. "We have a mystery, and it gets worse all the time."

"I think it gets better all the time," said Mike, swinging gently. 'Someday we will find out who made this swing and who lives here."

"We have plenty of time, and plenty of clues," said Benny. "Let me have a swing, too, Mike."

"No, you come another day and swing," said Lars suddenly. "We must get back to that bread-fruit."

When Lars took the breadfruit out of the fire, they saw some soft, baked fruit, the shape of enormous eggs. He took them out one by one and put them on big leaves.

"Those leaves are as big as umbrellas," said Jessie.

"Yes, people use them for umbrellas when it rains," said Lars. "Now see there are seeds inside the breadfruit." He took out about thirty seeds. Each was as big as a nut.

"Eat them," said Lars. "The seeds are nutty and rich. Then you eat the soft part of the fruit with the razor clam shells."

"We must make those spoons very soon," said Henry. "We need spoons for everything."

"I like this," said Benny. He bit into a seed. "It does taste nutty."

"I'll open the canned meat," said Henry. "Then we'll have meat and bread together."

He did so. With cold meat and hot breadfruit, the family enjoyed a full meal. They had bananas for dessert. They did not know that someone was watching them all the time.

The days went by very fast now. Every day brought more surprises. They made the two huts ready for rain, but it did not rain. Every day was

beautiful. The Blue Bay was bluer than ever, and the green bay was greener.

One day they all went to the spring for water. Benny looked first at the white shell. It had been moved.

Benny said to himself, "That shell has been moved. It was right next to this white stone. Now it is over on the other side. I bet someone drinks here every day."

But they never saw anyone. The myna bird did

not come back. They dug the sand out of the *Explorer II* boat and washed it. They pulled it higher on the sand. It looked fine. But this time they did not hear any whine from the treetops.

Everyone had a fine spoon now. They had bowls too. They made a bowl from half a coconut shell. Jessie said, "I like coconut milk better than dry milk now. It is sweeter."

"I like sugar cane the best," said Mike. "That is the sweetest of all."

"Sugar cane is our candy," said Benny. "We can pick it any time we want to."

And so the days went by. Nobody ever thought of the *Sea Star*, because they didn't want it to come. They were having too good a time.

CHAPTER 10

Trapped

One day Henry said suddenly, "I don't want a nap today."

"I don't either!' shouted Benny and Mike at the same time. "Let's walk over into the woods. It is cool enough there."

Mr. Alden laughed. He said, "I want a nap just the same."

Lars was fixing a hole in the roof of the girls' hut. "I think I'll stay home and work on the roof," he said. "You can explore if you want to. It is safe enough."

Henry said, "I'd like to see the other side of the island."

Lars nodded. He looked at Henry. "The best way to go is right behind the spring. When you get to the spring, you climb the rocks behind it. Then you go down the other side to the beach. There is nothing there but a beach."

"Good," said Henry. "Let's go!"

All the children jumped up. Off they started. Lars stopped his work to watch them. He said, "Fine children, Mr. Alden."

"Yes, they are," said Mr. Alden. "Every one of them."

Then Lars went back to his work. Mr. Alden went inside his hut to take a nap.

Very soon he came back to the door and looked up. He said, "I don't like to have the children go off alone, Lars. You know there is someone on this island. Just keep an eye on them, will you? Don't let them know."

Lars said quietly, "Yes, sir. I was going to follow

them in a minute. I don't want to spoil their fun. They will never know that I am watching."

"Good!" said Mr. Alden. "Thank you, Lars. I see that you understand what I mean. They always did like to be on their own."

The children walked happily through the ferns. Jessie said, "Isn't this fun, Henry? It's the first time we've been alone. It makes me think of the old days in the boxcar."

Henry smiled at his sister. "We had to plan everything for ourselves. Nobody helped us. It was fun."

"Did Jessie keep care of you, Ben?" asked Mike.

"*Take* care of me," said Benny.

"Now don't start that again!" cried Mike. "You know what I mean!"

"Yes," said Benny. "Everyone took care of me. I was young then. They taught me to read."

"Didn't you have to go to school?" asked Mike.

"Well, I did later," said Benny. "You and I had fun in school, Mike. We had a nice teacher. Now what was her name?"

"I don't remember," said Mike. "I just know she was nice. She was always telling us about bananas growing on trees. Think of that, Ben! And here we have really seen them growing."

"Her name made me think of cows," said Benny.

"Cows?" said Mike. "It didn't *me*. It was nothing like cows. I'm sure of that!"

The children soon came to the spring. They looked at the two beautiful little waterfalls for a minute. Henry looked at the rocks.

"That's a good climb," he said. "But I think we can all do it."

"We can start from the statue's nose," said Benny. He climbed up and sat down. Mike climbed up and sat on the statue's chin. They were very good seats.

"Some day I'd like to find the end of this statue," said Mike. "See if it has any feet."

"It is all covered with leaves and bushes," said Jessie. "But I'm sure we could find it."

"Not today, though," said Benny. "Today we are climbing this mountain."

Henry began to climb. "You all wait and see how I get along," he said.

Henry went up the rocks very well. Soon he called back, "Here is a nice big place half way up. We can stand here, or sit down and rest. Come along."

Mike said, "Now, Violet, I'll help you. Take my hand."

"Thank you, Mike," said Violet. "You are a better climber than I am."

Up they went. "Put your foot here, Violet," said Mike. "That's the last step. Then I'll pull you up."

Mike was very strong. He was very gentle with Violet. And at last they were all sitting on the wide rocks to rest.

But Benny could not sit still long. He turned and looked on every side. He turned around and looked behind him.

"Look," he said. "A stump!"

It was a stump. But it was not growing there.

Henry was excited. "Look, everyone!" he cried.

"That stump never grew up here. Someone put it here!"

"That's right," said Jessie. "See the stones on every side of it. The stones hold it."

"The stones keep it straight, so it won't fall off," said Benny.

Jessie said slowly, "I wonder what that stump is for."

"It must be to step on," said Benny.

"Benny, I think you are right!" cried Henry. "And I am going to step on it and see what I can see."

Henry put one foot on the stump very carefully. Then he lifted himself by a small tree.

"Well, what do you know!" he shouted.

"What is it?" cried Jessie.

"I can't believe my eyes," cried Henry. "It's a big cave. It is just like our old boxcar!"

"No!" said Jessie. "It can't be, Henry!"

"Well, it is," said Henry. "Way off here in the South Seas! Come up and see for yourself. You'll

have to take turns. Jessie, you come first. I'll come down."

Henry stepped off the stump. He gave Jessie his hand and up she went.

"Oh, Violet," she called. "It's a tall wide cave in the rocks. It's very long, and the floor is a bed. It is all covered with leaves and ferns. And Henry, did you see the shelf?"

"Yes, I certainly did," said Henry. "That is how I was sure it was like the boxcar. It has dishes on it."

"What kind of dishes, Jessie?" called Benny. He could hardly wait for his turn.

"Well, there is a pile of shells for plates. I'll come down, now. Benny ought to see these dishes."

Violet said, "Let Benny have my turn."

Benny was glad. He got up on the stump. Henry helped him. Then Benny saw something that made him more excited than ever.

"My pink cup!" he shouted. "It is like my pink cup!"

"I think so too," said Jessie. "I think someone made this place to sleep in."

"I think someone made it to live in when it rains," said Henry. "And this has a wide roof where the rocks come out over the cave."

"Let me try it!" said Mike. "I'll climb in and lie down."

Benny came down. Mike went up. He lay down on the bed.

"Oh, it's as hard as a rock. I could never sleep here!" he cried.

"You might if you had to," said Henry. "Suppose it was pouring rain outside."

Benny climbed down as far as the statue's nose. He sat down and watched Mike. Suddenly Benny saw the trees move above him. First one tree moved. Then another. Benny thought, "Some animal is jumping from one tree to another."

Without a word, he followed the trees. He crashed through the bushes and ferns. He kept looking up. All the time he watched the tree tops moving.

"Yes," he thought, "somebody jumps from one tree to the next. Maybe it's a monkey. But this time I'm going to find out!"

On went Benny. He was so excited that he fell down twice. He picked himself up and crashed on. On and on went the thing in the trees. On and on went Benny. He never thought of the cave now. All he thought of was the mystery.

"Is it ever going to stop?" he thought. He was out of breath. The bushes and ferns were much bigger than he was. "I won't stop! I won't stop till *it* does!"

But he did. He put his foot down and everything gave way under him. Down he fell. As he fell, he thought, "Hope there is no water in this!"

But no, the hole was deep, and dry. "I'm glad!" thought Benny. "But now how do I get out? I'd better yell. I hope Henry can hear me!"

Benny did not have time to make a sound. Over the edge of the hole he saw a boy, very thin and brown, with long hair.

"Who are you?" asked Benny looking up.

"I'm Peter," said the boy.

"Oh, you look like a girl!" said Benny. "Long hair!"

"No, I'm a boy," said Peter. "I can't cut my hair with my knife. Come on, now, Benny. Give me your hand."

Benny took hold of the brown hand. He thought it would be soft like a girl's, but it was very hard like a dog's paw.

Peter pulled Benny out of the hole. "That hole is my store house," said Peter. "It is a trap, too."

"So I see," said Benny. "How do you know I'm Benny?"

"Oh, I've watched you for a long time. I know you all," said Peter.

The two boys sat down and looked at each other. They never thought of the family back at the cave.

CHAPTER 11

Peter

Back at the cave, Mike was saying, "You can have another turn, Ben. I'm coming down."

But of course Benny did not answer. He was not there.

"Goodness!" cried Jessie. "Where is Benny?"

They began to call, "Benny! Benny!" They all listened.

"I hear a funny noise over that way," said Violet, pointing. "It sounds like Benny! He is in trouble!"

The children crashed through the bushes and over rocks. They were calling "Benny!" all the time. And suddenly right before their eyes they saw a strange sight. Benny and a stranger were sitting on the edge of a deep hole.

"Oh, Benny, are you hurt?" cried Jessie.

"Not at all," said Benny. "This is Peter! I fell into his trap and he pulled me out."

Henry came and sat down by the boys. He said to Peter, "Have you been all alone on this island?"

"Yes," said Peter. "I've been alone for about three weeks."

"Three weeks!" cried Henry. "How do you know?"

"I cut some marks in a tree. Mr. Anderson was with me at first. He cut the marks for six months. So after he went, I cut them myself. One every day."

"Who was Mr. Anderson?" asked Jessie.

"He was a sailor," said the boy. "Our ship hit a reef and went down. I was in a lifeboat with Mr. Anderson and we came to this island. We were together for six months, and Mr. Anderson went swimming and I never saw him again."

"So you have been here almost seven months," said Jessie.

"That's right," said Peter.

"How in the world do you get along alone?" asked Jessie.

"Oh, I get along fine," said Peter. "I do just what Mr. Anderson did."

"Tell me something, Peter," said Mike. "How did you happen to make your bed in the cave?"

"I thought it would be fun," said Peter. "Once I read about some children who were all alone. Then it rained so hard, I had to get somewhere out of the rain. Those rocks make a fine roof. I used to sit and watch the rain before you came to the island."

Henry whispered to Benny. "Don't tell him about us now. Later you can."

Mike looked at Peter and said, "Did you take our crackers that day?"

Peter looked upset. "I am sorry about that," he said. "I have been here so long, and everything was free. I could take anything I wanted. Bananas, fish, coconuts, oysters, crabs and sugar cane. When I saw the crackers I took those, too."

"It's all right," said Mike. "Nobody thinks I took them now."

Henry said, "Peter, why didn't you call out to us before? Were you afraid of us?"

"Yes, I was," said Peter. "Mr. Anderson said I

must keep very still if I saw anyone on this island. I mustn't let anyone know I was here."

"I suppose he meant dangerous men like cannibals," said Henry. "But there aren't any more cannibals around here."

"I didn't know," said Peter. "You might be dangerous! I have watched you for a long time, and now I know you are all right."

"A good thing we found you!" said Henry.

"We know you can take care of yourself," said Jessie. "But you can live with us and have some of our food. And we are going away soon. Don't you want to go along?"

"Yes, I do," said Peter. "I miss my father and mother. I used to live near Boston."

"We'll take you to Boston," said Benny. "Just as soon as our ship comes. And we'll find your mother and father for you."

"Here, old fellow!" said Henry. "Don't promise! We'll try. And if anyone can find your parents, Grandfather can."

Mike said, "Look how brown you are, Peter."

"Oh, I'm just sunburned. I have been living in the sun for so long."

"Come on, Peter," said Henry. "We'll take you to see Lars and my grandfather."

Peter did not ask who they were, because he knew very well. He said, "I watched you the day you came to the island. My, I was scared when I saw the ship! I watched you when you found the turtle shell. I heard every word you said. I watched you find my boat, and I was afraid you would take my boat away."

"Yes, we heard you whine and moan," said Benny. "I thought someone was in trouble and it was you."

The family began to walk back to the houses. Jessie said, "Didn't you almost forget how to talk, Peter?"

"Oh, I always talked to myself," said Peter. "I talked all day, until you came. And then I had my bird to talk to."

"What can he say?" asked Mike.

"*She,*" said Peter. "Old Myna is a girl. She says 'Good morning' and 'Good night' and 'Hello, Peter,' and 'Thank you' and 'Yes' and 'No' and 'Happy Birthday' and 'Look out, it's hot!' "

"I can see she is quite a talker," said Henry. "She must be a lot of company for you."

"Yes, I love old Myna. That's her name, because Mr. Anderson said it was a myna bird."

"Isn't it better to have people for company, Peter?" asked Violet.

"Oh, yes," said Peter. "That is why I came to help Benny out of my trap. I thought the time had come. And you were all alone without the others."

"It's wonderful," said Jessie. "Won't Grandfather and Lars be surprised!"

But just then Lars was going very fast and very quietly back to the house. When the children came home, Lars was sitting there on the top of the hut still fixing the roof.

"Lars!" shouted Benny. "See what we found! Our Mystery!"

Lars looked up and saw Peter. "Oh, a boy!" Lars said. "Where did you find him? Mr. Alden! Come and see this boy!"

Mr. Alden came to the door and looked out.

"It's Peter, Grandfather!" said Henry. "He has lived here for six months!"

Mr. Alden tried to wake up. He thought he was dreaming. He said, "Six months! How could he?"

"He lived just the way we do," said Benny. "Only he never had any crackers or milk or meat."

Lars said, "Now, Peter, come and sit down and tell us about this. Did you come in that lifeboat that is all filled with sand?"

"Yes, sir," said Peter. "Mr. Anderson and I came in it six months ago."

Lars and Mr. Alden looked at each other.

Then Mr. Alden came and sat down too. He said, "Peter, I'd like to know more about the shipwreck. I suppose it was a shipwreck. Can you bear to tell me?"

"Oh, yes," said Peter. "I'd *like* to. Maybe it won't

seem so bad if I tell somebody. There was a terrible storm in the middle of the night. We were all seasick. Then the ship hit a reef and began to go down. The sailors got three lifeboats over the side. I was in one with my mother and father and Mr. Anderson. Then some others got in and the boat tipped over. Everybody went into the water. I couldn't see a thing."

"Do you think your parents were saved?" asked Mr. Alden gently.

"I don't know," said Peter. "Maybe. But it was very dark, you know. I was going down. Suddenly I felt Mr. Anderson lifting me into a boat again. When I woke up, I was here. We never saw any other boat after that."

"Your parents think you were lost, then," said Grandfather.

"Yes, I'm sure they do, if they were saved."

Lars said, "Some people got picked up, because the paper said they were taken to San Francisco."

"Is that so?" said Peter. He looked at Lars quickly. "Maybe my father and mother were saved. But they would never know about me. Mr. Anderson and I never saw any ship."

"The wreck must have been quite far away," said Grandfather.

"Yes, it was, because Mr. Anderson told me he rowed a whole day and a night. I didn't think anyone would ever come. I wish you would cut my hair!"

"Henry can cut hair very well," said Mike.

Violet took her scissors out of her workbag and gave them to Henry.

Henry began to cut. He said, "You'd better save this long hair, Peter. Someday you'll like to see it." Then he cut Peter's hair like Mike's.

"You look fine now," said Henry.

"You did well to live alone, Peter," said Lars. "I think you are very brave."

"I had to be," said Peter. "I'm sorry about my clothes. Don't they look terrible?"

Everyone had noticed what Peter was wearing. He looked very strange. He was wearing lots of big leaves that were tied with brown strings. And many more brown strings hung down.

"I got some strings off coconuts," said Peter, "and I tied leaves together. One time I lost a button when I washed my clothes. Then they just wore out."

Mike got up. He ran down to the box. He came back at once and held out his hand to Peter.

Peter took one look. Then he cried, "My button! I lost it in a pool right down there!" He pointed. "I never could find it."

"You couldn't find it, because our fish ate it," said Mike. "Then we ate the fish."

"May I have my button?" asked Peter. "I'd love to keep it."

Grandfather got up. "Yes, Peter, keep it," he said. "Henry, go and fix up some of your clothes for Peter. He will feel better, if he looks better."

The two boys went into the house at once. Soon they came back. Peter looked like a different boy.

Henry said to Lars, "When do you think the *Sea Star* will come back?"

"Well, well!" said Lars. "This is the first time anyone has said one word about the *Sea Star!* She may come any time now."

Jessie said, "You see we didn't want to leave Blue Bay. And now we do. We want to find Peter's father and mother."

"I've almost forgotten what they look like," said Peter. "But I will know them!"

Grandfather said quietly, "What is your last name, Peter? Peter what?"

"Horn," said Peter.

"Horn!" shouted Mike and Benny at once.

"Our teacher!" said Benny. "That was our teacher's name, too. I *knew* it made me think of *cows*."

"Cows?" asked Jessie. "What are you talking about?"

"Well, cows have horns," said Benny.

"Oh, dear!" laughed Jessie. "You are the funniest boy!"

"Peter Horn," said Mr. Alden slowly. He was thinking.

"My father's name is Peter Horn, too," said Peter.

"That will help, my boy," said Mr. Alden. "We'll try to find them. But you understand they may not be alive, don't you?"

"Oh, yes," said Peter. "I was just thinking what would I do, if we went home, and we didn't find them."

"Don't worry about that, Peter," said Henry. "You can live with us and be part of our family."

Peter could not believe his eyes when everyone smiled and nodded—even Mr. Alden himself.

CHAPTER 12

Eight in the Family

Grandfather was thinking. He said, "Benny, you must not think that Peter's mother is your teacher, just because she had the same name. There are many people named Horn."

Lars said, "What happened to Mr. Anderson?"

"I don't know," said Peter. "He said he was going swimming near a sandy beach, but he never came back."

"Do you mean a very green bay?" asked Mike.

"No, I mean the one on the other side of it, where the boat is."

Nobody said a word. But everyone thought, "Shark Bay! How lucky we were to have Lars with us!"

Jessie said suddenly, "Are you hungry, Peter?"

"Not very," said Peter. "But you do have some more crackers, don't you? You see they make me think of bread. I haven't had any bread for six months."

"Six months!" cried Violet.

"That's why I took the crackers, Mr. Lars," said Peter.

"That's all right," said Lars. "Don't worry."

"I did worry," said Peter, "when I saw you were blaming that other boy."

"Me," said Mike.

"Yes, Mike, I am awfully sorry."

"Think nothing of it!" said Mike. "Come on, Ben!"

The two boys raced for the sea biscuit. It was such fun to see Peter eat crackers. He seemed half starved.

"Wait till you see what we have for supper," said Benny. We're going to have stew and a pudding!"

"A pudding? Oh, yes, I remember what a pudding is," said Peter. He stopped eating for a minute. "A pudding is sweet."

"Yes," said Mike. "Ours is made of coconut milk, sugar cane, and bananas."

"Sounds good," said Peter. "My mother used to cook good things. I hope we can find her."

"Well, if Grandfather can't find her, nobody can," said Benny. "He has ways."

Mike said suddenly. "You can have my blanket, Peter."

Peter said, "You are a very kind boy, Mike. But I wouldn't know what to do with a blanket. I can sleep on a rock. I am hard all over."

"You must show us how to climb trees," said Henry.

"It's easy," said Peter, "if there is something you want at the top of the tree."

Mr. Alden was listening to all this. He was wide

awake now. He watched Peter carefully. "A good boy," he thought. "Just think of one of our children living here for six months!" He shook himself. He had a plan which he did not tell to anyone. But he told them all, "Now we have eight in the family."

It was a happy family at supper. Lars gave his spoon to Peter. He took the big cooking spoon himself. They all began to eat meat stew.

All at once a voice said, "Look out, it's hot!"

"Who said that?" cried Mike.

"It's old Myna," said Peter. He made a funny

noise with his mouth and down flew a dark purple bird. It had white on its wings and orange on its head.

"Hello, Myna," said Peter.

"Hello, Peter," said Myna.

"Oh, make him say something about me!" begged Mike.

"*Her*," said Peter. He took the bird on his finger and said, "Myna, say 'What's the matter, Mike?' "

The bird said nothing.

"She won't talk for us," said Benny. "She is afraid."

"Oh, no, she's not afraid," said Peter. "She has to study every new word."

Peter said it again two or three times. He fed the bird a piece of meat.

"Look out, it's hot!" said Myna. Then she went right along without stopping, "What's the matter, Mike?"

Mike was delighted. "What a talker!" he said "Maybe we could teach her to sing."

"Oh, she can sing already," said Peter. "Myna, sing 'My country, 'tis of thee.'" He hummed it.

Sure enough, Myna sang it right after him.

"She's wonderful," said Henry.

"She's got a funny voice when she sings," said Mike.

"So have some people," said Benny. "Her singing voice is different."

Henry said, "Soon we'll have to think about the ship's coming. I mean get our things ready. My shoes are almost worn out."

"I never had any shoes here," said Peter. "I didn't have time to put them on the night the ship was wrecked. Feel my feet, Benny."

Benny did so. "Oh, your feet are as hard as rocks! Really, Henry, feel them."

Henry said, "Yes, they are just like a dog's foot. You have been climbing trees and rocks for so long, Peter. It will be terrible for you to wear shoes."

"Yes, but I'd like some new shoes," said Peter. "I used to dream of having new shoes."

Then they tried the pudding. It was delicious.

When supper was over, Peter began to teach them to climb trees. "Oh, you have to take off your shoes," he said.

Henry tried it a few times, and did very well. "It is much easier without shoes. Soon my feet will be as hard as yours, Peter."

"That will take a long time!" said Peter. "And I hope we won't stay here that long."

When they went to bed that night, old Myna went to sleep first. For the first time in three weeks, nobody was watching from the trees.

Out on the great ocean the *Sea Star* was coming nearer and nearer. Captain Brown smiled to himself. He laughed when he thought of Benny and Mike. He didn't know that there was another boy now, named Peter Horn.

CHAPTER 13

Sea Star

Old Myna woke up first. She hopped out of the house and flew into the trees. She ate her breakfast and waited for the sun to come up. Then she began to call, "Wake up, sleepyhead!"

It woke everyone. Benny laughed. "That's old Myna. She sounds like a real person."

Lars and Henry went down to start the fire. "How Grandfather does enjoy his coffee!" said Henry as they walked along.

"Not more than I do!" said Lars, laughing. "That little girl Violet thinks of everybody."

"Yes, she does," said Henry. "Now, what do you think about Peter's parents? Do you think they are alive?"

"Who knows?" said Lars. "Some people were saved. They could be Peter's parents. Your grandfather will find them if they are alive."

"Yes, Grandfather is quite wonderful," said Henry.

They were talking so hard that they never looked at the sea. They knelt down to build the fire. Along came the *Sea Star* just the same, nearer and nearer, but nobody saw it as it steamed along.

Just as the coffee began to boil over, Mr. Alden shouted, "Hey, Lars!"

They looked up. Mr. Alden was laughing and pointing out to sea.

"The ship!" cried Henry. "The *Sea Star!*"

Benny and Mike came racing down to the beach. They danced around on the sand and waved their arms.

"They can't see you," said Henry.

"Very soon they can," said Lars. "I wish we had a bigger coffeepot. For company."

Jessie said, "Never mind, Lars. They have coffee on the ship. Go ahead and drink this."

"Who will come in the lifeboat, Lars? Will it be Captain Brown?"

"No, I don't think Captain Brown will leave his ship. I think it will be the Second Mate."

Lars was wrong that time. The *Sea Star* stopped outside Blue Bay and let down a boat. In the boat were the Second Mate and Captain Brown himself.

As the boat came up with the waves, all the men pulled it up on the sand.

"Well, Captain, this is good of you to come yourself!" said Mr. Alden.

Then the Captain saw Peter. "*Where* did this boy come from?" he cried.

"He was on the *Explorer II*, sir!" said Lars. "Been here ever since the wreck."

"We're going to find his parents," said Benny. "Grandfather is."

"Now, Benny," said Henry.

"*Maybe* he is," said Benny. "If he can, and he always can."

The Captain looked at Mr. Alden. He started to say something.

Mr. Alden said quickly, "Let's all sit down. Then we can talk. Have some breakfast?"

"Thanks. We just ate aboard ship," said the Captain. "We'll watch you."

"Oh, we've had a neat time," said Benny. "But we want to go home, now."

"Yes, we do," said Mr. Alden. "Start back to San Francisco right away. I want to help this boy find his parents. Do you all want to go home?"

"Oh, *yes!*" said Jessie. "Oh, *yes!*" said Violet.

Peter said nothing. But his eyes were very bright.

"Peter's going to cry," thought Benny.

But Peter did not cry. He went over to Mr. Alden and held out his hand. Mr. Alden took it.

"And now *Grandfather's* going to cry," thought Benny.

But Mr. Alden did not cry, either. He just said, "Hard as a rock! What a hard hand! But maybe hard work kept you happy. Work is good. Remember that, my boy."

"How long will it take you to get ready, sir?" asked the Captain.

"Not long," said Benny. "We haven't anything to pack."

"Not so fast, my boy," said Mr. Alden. "You surely want to take Mike's turtle-kettle. And we must take our plates and spoons."

"Let's take Peter's dishes, too," said Jessie.

"And old Myna," said Peter.

"Oh, yes, old Myna," said Henry. "Can you catch her, Peter?"

"I can catch her, but she won't like the ship. She will fly away."

"How about that, Captain?" asked Mr. Alden. "Have you a bird cage?"

"No. But I have a crab trap."

Mr. Alden went on. "Another thing, Captain, have you your secret camera?"

"Oh, yes, I always have that."

"Well, Henry will go with you, and you take some pictures of the waterfalls and the spring, and the statue—"

"And Peter's cave," said Benny.

"Yes, surely. Get a picture of that, close up. Then take the *Explorer II* lifeboat, and be sure to get the name on it."

"Then come back and take a picture of our huts and one of all of us!" said Jessie.

"I'll take that now," said the Captain, laughing. "Stand close together."

Just before he took the picture, down flew old Myna. So Peter had the bird on his finger in the picture, and everyone was laughing.

Off went Henry and the Captain. Lars began to pack the boxes. "You boys can help me," he said.

"I'm too homesick!" cried Mike. "I don't want to leave Blue Bay! Oh, I don't want to go home!"

"Yes, you do!" cried Benny. He jumped up and said, "More coffee, Grandfather?"

"Thank you, Benny. The last drop is the best. Come here, Mike."

Mike went over. He put his hand on Mr. Alden's knee. He said, "I've had a beautiful time, Mr. Alden. I don't want it to end."

"Let me talk to you, Mike. It isn't going to end. Think of taking Peter home. You will always have a good time, my boy. Just take things as they come. Remember I will always help you. Try to like everything, even ends."

"I'll try," said Mike. "I do like most things."

"I know you do. Good boy!"

Mike went to work then, filling boxes. "I hope those pictures come out right, Ben," he said. "Won't it be fun to look at them when we are at home!"

Soon everything was packed. Henry and the Captain came back and took a picture of the two huts.

"All packed except old Myna," said Jessie.

The Second Mate put the crab trap on the sand. Peter put a berry inside and Myna walked in. Peter shut the door.

"Neat!" said Benny.

Lars put out the fire with sea water. Then the men pulled both boats down to the water.

"I'll take Mr. Alden with me," said the Captain. He winked at Mike. "We want to talk."

"Well," said Benny, "that's all right. We want to talk, too!"

CHAPTER 14

Home

As the two boats went through Blue Bay, Captain Brown took a picture of the beach. He said, "That will show the fireplace and the two houses. And now I am ready to make any plans you want to, Mr. Alden."

"Well, first, maybe Peter's parents were *not* saved. But I will do everything to find out. So this is my plan."

By the time the boats reached the *Sea Star*, the plan was made. The crew was waiting at the rail. They were all laughing. They helped the family out of the lifeboat and carried the turtle-kettle up on the deck. The Captain went at once to the radio room.

Mr. Alden sat down and looked all around. "Oh, another cup of coffee!" he said. He took it from the sailor. "Thanks very much."

"Just think of having a saucer!" said Benny. "Oh, Grandfather, he's bringing some toast!"

The children looked hard at the toast. "*Buttered* toast!" yelled Mike. He could hardly get the words out.

Mr. Alden looked at Peter. Then he began to count, "—one, two, three, four, five,—six with Lars. Will you bring a whole loaf of buttered toast, please?" he said. "These children would like lots of bread and butter. Think of that!"

When it came, Peter looked at it. "I can't believe it," he said. But when the Captain came back, all the children ate as if they were starved.

"That's all we want," said Henry. "Bread."

Peter said, "I'll never eat bread again without being thankful."

Then Mr. Alden said, "After this, don't go into the radio room. You used to go and talk with Bill. But now, *don't*."

The Captain noticed that nobody said "Why?" He thought, "And that's all there is to it! I wish all people behaved as well as that."

The *Sea Star* was going at full speed. Bill went in and out of the radio room very often. He always took a yellow paper to Mr. Alden. Grandfather would say a few words and Bill would go back.

"Now we'll show you the ship, Peter," said Benny.

When they all came back on deck Grandfather said, "Your lessons begin again this afternoon. Even Peter! And this time, you will each *write* a book. About this trip."

"Write a book!" cried Jessie. "What fun!"

"Write a book?" said Mike. "I can't write a book!"

"You'll have to, if Grandfather says so, Mikey old boy!" said Benny. "I'll bet your book will be the best and funniest of all."

It was. Mike kept them all laughing as he read each page.

The children kept busy, but they longed to get home. After many days, a loud bell rang. All the children jumped up and ran up on deck.

"I thought that loud bell would get you!" said Grandfather. "Good news, Peter!"

"You mean Peter's father?" whispered Mike.

"Yes! His father and mother are alive. They will

be waiting for us at the dock in San Francisco."

"Oh, my!" said Peter.

"Now you can all read the radiograms. The last one just came. It says, 'Son Peter Horn last seen in lifeboat from *Explorer II*.'"

"My own father sent that?" asked Peter.

"Yes, he signs his name, Peter Horn."

Henry put his arm around Peter and said, "Come on, old boy, and sit down on the bench." Benny and Mike sat down on the other side.

"And we land tomorrow!" said Mr. Alden.

"I hope I can live till tomorrow," said Benny.

They all lived till "tomorrow." They were very much excited when they began to see land. San Francisco came nearer and nearer. They went under the Golden Gate bridge. Soon they saw the dock. There were crowds of people waiting for ships.

"Oh, dear," said Jessie. "I suppose we must say goodby to the crew."

They all shook hands with Captain Brown and the sailors. But then they came to Lars.

Violet looked up at Lars and said, "How can we say goodby to you, Lars?"

Mike said, "Maybe we'll never see you again."

But Lars smiled at Violet and said, "You'll see me again, all right. I often come your way."

"Come to dinner!" said Benny. "Come any time! We'll have beans for you!"

Just then Peter began to shout, "Oh, I see my mother! And my father! There they are, waving!"

"Is that your mother?" yelled Benny. "It's not our teacher! It doesn't look a bit like her."

"I was sure you boys would be disappointed about that," said Grandfather.

"I don't care," said Benny. "The neat thing is that she's Peter's mother!"

At last they were all on the dock.

"Hi! Mother!" cried Peter.

"I thought I would never see you again!" said Mrs. Horn.

Mr. Horn took Peter's hand to help him up the steps to the street.

"Don't help Peter, Mr. Horn," said Mike. He laughed. "Peter can climb right up the side of a house!"

Peter was not too happy wearing shoes. But he did very well.

Mr. Alden looked at Mr. Horn. He said, "Let's go to some quiet place! We'll have lunch, and then we'll all take the plane east."

"I never can thank you enough for bringing Peter home!" said Mr. Horn.

"Don't try," said Mr. Alden. "Here are some taxis. Everyone get in."

Very soon they were all sitting at a big table for lunch. "Oh, *peanut butter!*" cried Benny. "I thought I'd never see *you* again!"

"Is that what you want?" asked Mr. Alden. He laughed. All of them wanted peanut butter. "Think of that, Mr. Horn," he said. "They want peanut butter, when they can have almost anything in the world."

Peter's father and mother were told all about Blue

Bay. Peter's mother said, "At last we have found Peter. I never really gave up hope of finding him."

"Grandfather finds lots of things," said Benny. "Now where will Peter live?"

"Peter will live near Boston. This is a picture of our house," said Mr. Horn. He took out a picture.

"A nice little place!" said Mike. "Nice trees to climb, but no banana trees."

"No," said Mr. Horn laughing. "We have no banana trees."

After lunch they all took the plane. Everyone on the plane smiled to see the happy group. They talked all the time. Mike and Benny walked up and down. They told the passengers about the island, and all about Peter.

Mike did not want to get off at Chicago. But when he saw his mother and his brother Pat, he changed his mind.

"And my *teacher!*" he yelled. "My teacher came to meet me! I bet she doesn't know that bananas grow up and not down!"

TERMINAL
BENNY

"That's our Mike for you!" said Henry. He patted Mike's shoulder. "Next year you will be teaching your teachers, Mike."

At last the plane landed in Boston. They all got off the plane. Then they had to say goodby to Peter.

"We'll come to see you often," said Henry.

Mr. Horn carried old Myna's cage. Old Myna said, "What's the matter, Mike?"

Benny laughed and laughed. He said, "That shows that old Myna doesn't know what she says. She just talks."

"Mike's gone," said Myna. She looked right at Benny.

"What do you know!" said Henry.

"What do you know!" said Myna.

"Let's go, Mother," said Peter. "Next thing old Myna will say, 'Look out, it's hot!' "

"Well, it is hot, sure enough," said Benny.

They all watched Peter go out of the door of the airport.

Henry took a long breath. He said, "Grandfather,

we can never thank you enough for this wonderful trip."

"Don't try, my boy," said Mr. Alden. "I had a pretty good time myself." The Alden family reached home. Watch began to bark. He was so glad to see his family again. Mr. Alden began to sing, "East, west, home is best."

Benny hugged Watch. He said, "Well, that's right, Grandfather. Home is best. But Blue Bay was pretty neat, too. Let's go somewhere else next year."

Mr. Alden smiled at Benny. But all he said was, "Maybe."

The children were very happy. They all knew that with Grandfather, *maybe* almost always meant *yes.*

GERTRUDE CHANDLER WARNER discovered when she was teaching that many readers who like an exciting story could find no books that were both easy and fun to read. She decided to try to meet this need, and her first book, *The Boxcar Children*, quickly proved she had succeeded.

Miss Warner drew on her own experiences to write the mystery. As a child she spent hours watching trains go by on the tracks opposite her family home. She often dreamed about what it would be like to set up housekeeping in a caboose or freight car—the situation the Alden children find themselves in.

When Miss Warner received requests for more adventures involving Henry, Jessie, Violet, and Benny Alden, she began additional stories. In each, she chose a special setting and introduced unusual or eccentric characters who liked the unpredictable.

While the mystery element is central to each of Miss Warner's books, she never thought of them as strictly juvenile mysteries. She liked to stress the Aldens' independence and resourcefulness and their solid New England devotion to using up and making do. The Aldens go about most of their adventures with as little adult supervision as possible—something else that delights young readers.

Miss Warner lived in Putnam, Connecticut, until her death in 1979. During her lifetime, she received hundreds of letters from girls and boys telling her how much they liked her books. And so she continued the Aldens' adventures, writing a total of nineteen books in the Boxcar Children series.